BATTLE EXTRAVAGONZO #3

ABDO
Spotlight

DARK HORSE BOOKS

PopCap

Written by **PAUL TOBIN**

Art by **TIM LATTIE**

Colors by **MATT J. RAINWATER**

Letters by **STEVE DUTRO**

Cover by **RON CHAN**

President and Publisher **MIKE RICHARDSON**
Editor **PHILIP R. SIMON**
Assistant Editor **MEGAN WALKER**
Designer **BRENNAN THOME**
Digital Art Technician **CHRISTINA McKENZIE**

Special thanks to Leigh Beach, A.J. Rathbun, Kristen Star, Jeremy Vanhoozer, and everyone at PopCap Games.

DarkHorse.com
PopCap.com

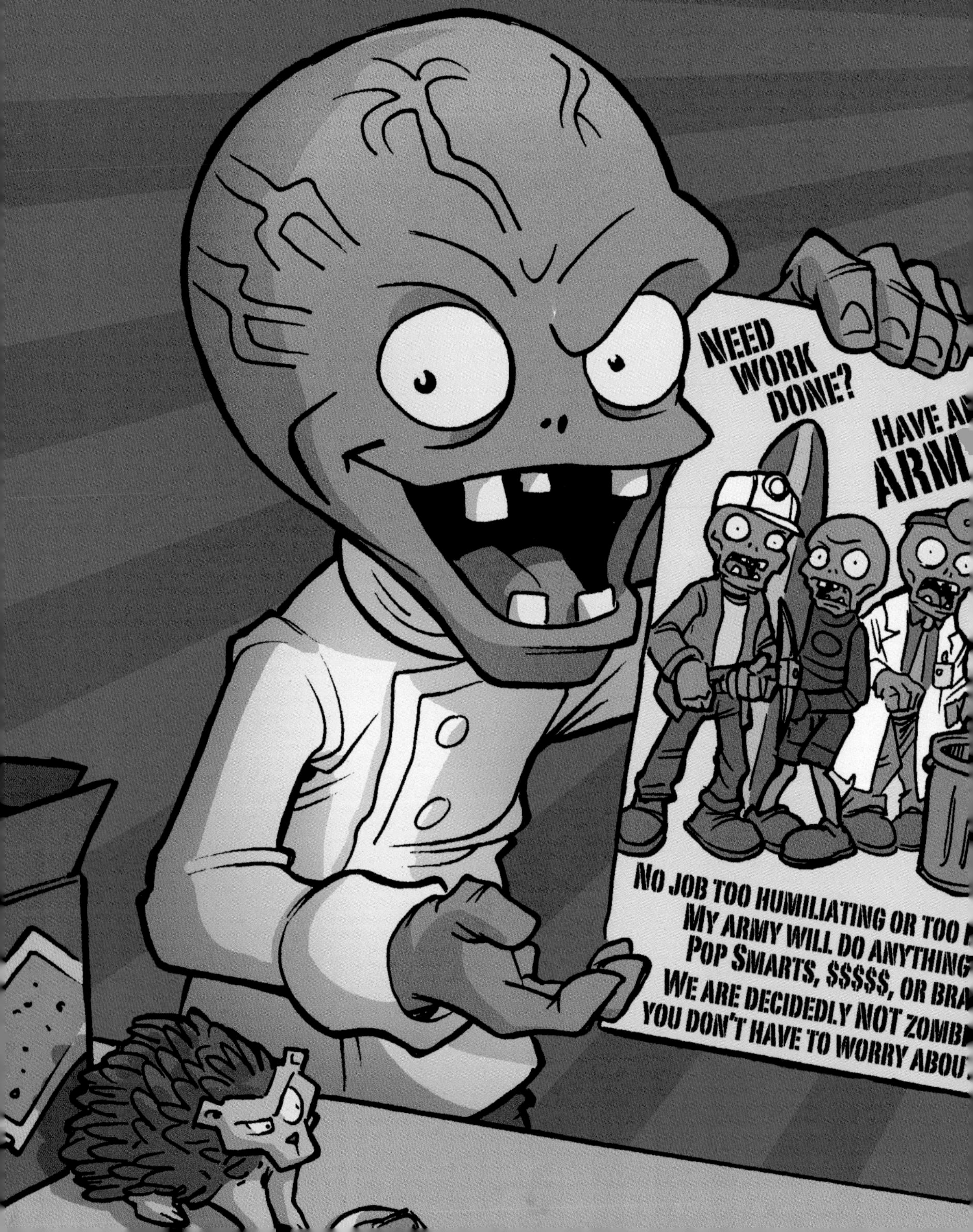
NEED WORK DONE?
NO JOB TOO HUMILIATING OR TOO
MY ARMY WILL DO ANYTHING
POP SMARTS, $$$$$, OR
WE ARE DECIDEDLY NOT
YOU DON'T HAVE TO WORRY

PLANTS vs. ZOMBIES

BATTLE EXTRAVAGONZO #3

ABDOBOOKS.COM

Reinforced library bound edition published in 2020 by Spotlight, a division of ABDO, PO Box 398166, Minneapolis, Minnesota 55439. Spotlight produces high-quality reinforced library bound editions for schools and libraries.
Published by agreement with Dark Horse Comics.

Printed in the United States of America, North Mankato, Minnesota.
042019
092019

THIS BOOK CONTAINS RECYCLED MATERIALS

Library of Congress Control Number: 2019938226

Publisher's Cataloging-in-Publication Data

Names: Tobin, Paul, author. | Lattie, Tim, illustrator.
Title: Battle extravagonzo / writer: Paul Tobin; art: Tim Lattie.
Description: Minneapolis, Minnesota: Spotlight, 2020 | Series: Plants vs. zombies
Summary: The Battle Extravagonzo is on as Zomboss and Crazy Dave compete to buy the same factory at the center of Neighborville.
Identifiers: ISBN 9781532143809 (#1 ; lib. bdg.) | ISBN 9781532143816 (#2 ; lib. bdg.) | ISBN 9781532143823 (#3 ; lib. bdg.)
Subjects: LCSH: Plants vs. zombies (Game)--Juvenile fiction. | Plants--Juvenile fiction. | Zombies--Juvenile fiction. | Battles--Juvenile fiction. | Graphic novels--Juvenile fiction. | Comic books, strips, etc--Juvenile fiction.
Classification: DDC 741.5--dc23

Spotlight

A Division of ABDO
abdobooks.com

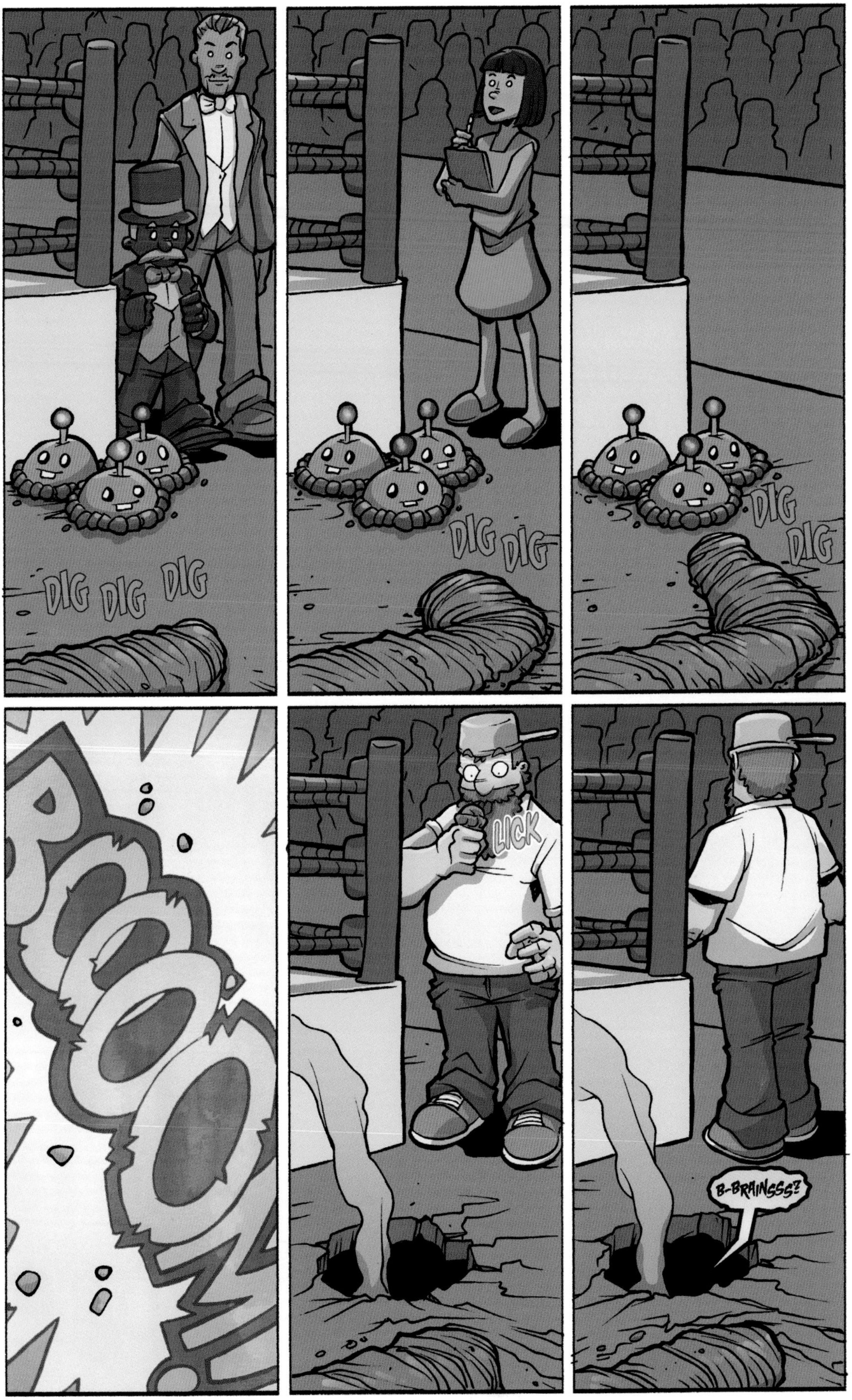
DIG DIG DIG
DIG DIG
DIG DIG
LICK
B-BRAINSSS?

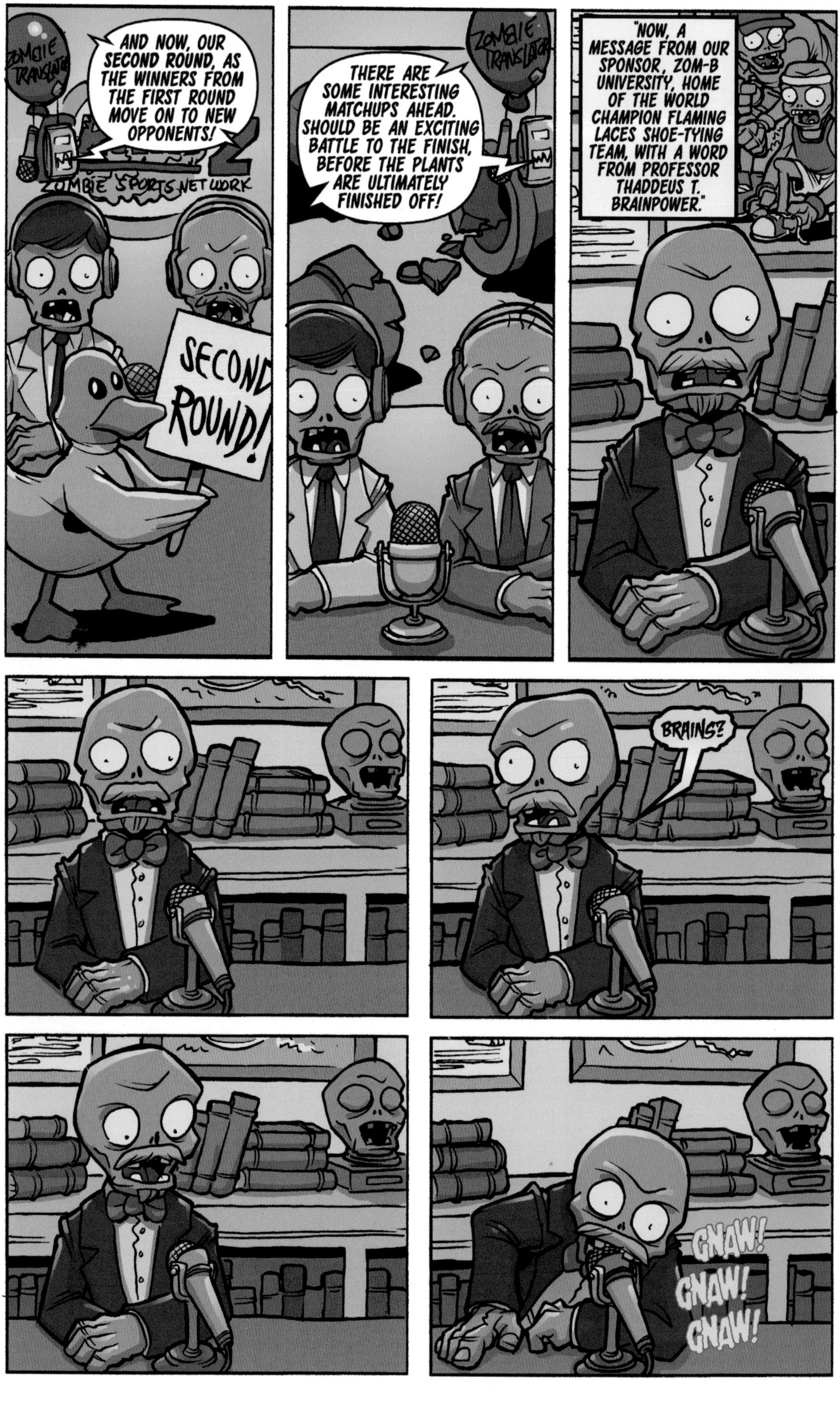
ZOMBIE TRANSLATOR
AND NOW, OUR SECOND ROUND, AS THE WINNERS FROM THE FIRST ROUND MOVE ON TO NEW OPPONENTS!
ZOMBIE SPORTS NETWORK
SECOND ROUND!
ZOMBIE TRANSLATOR
THERE ARE SOME INTERESTING MATCHUPS AHEAD. SHOULD BE AN EXCITING BATTLE TO THE FINISH, BEFORE THE PLANTS ARE ULTIMATELY FINISHED OFF!
"NOW, A MESSAGE FROM OUR SPONSOR, ZOM-B UNIVERSITY, HOME OF THE WORLD CHAMPION FLAMING LACES SHOE-TYING TEAM, WITH A WORD FROM PROFESSOR THADDEUS T. BRAINPOWER."
BRAINS?
GNAW!
GNAW!
GNAW!

LET THE FIGHTS...BEGIN AGAIN!

HYPNO-SHROOM VS. MR. STUBBINS

Second Round... Fight!

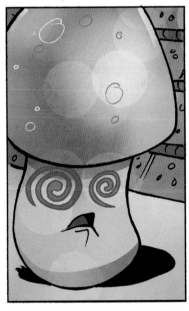

GLINT GLEAM GLINT

BRRRUMMu

GLINT GLEAM GLINT

??

REFLECT!

!!

Mr. Stubbins wins!

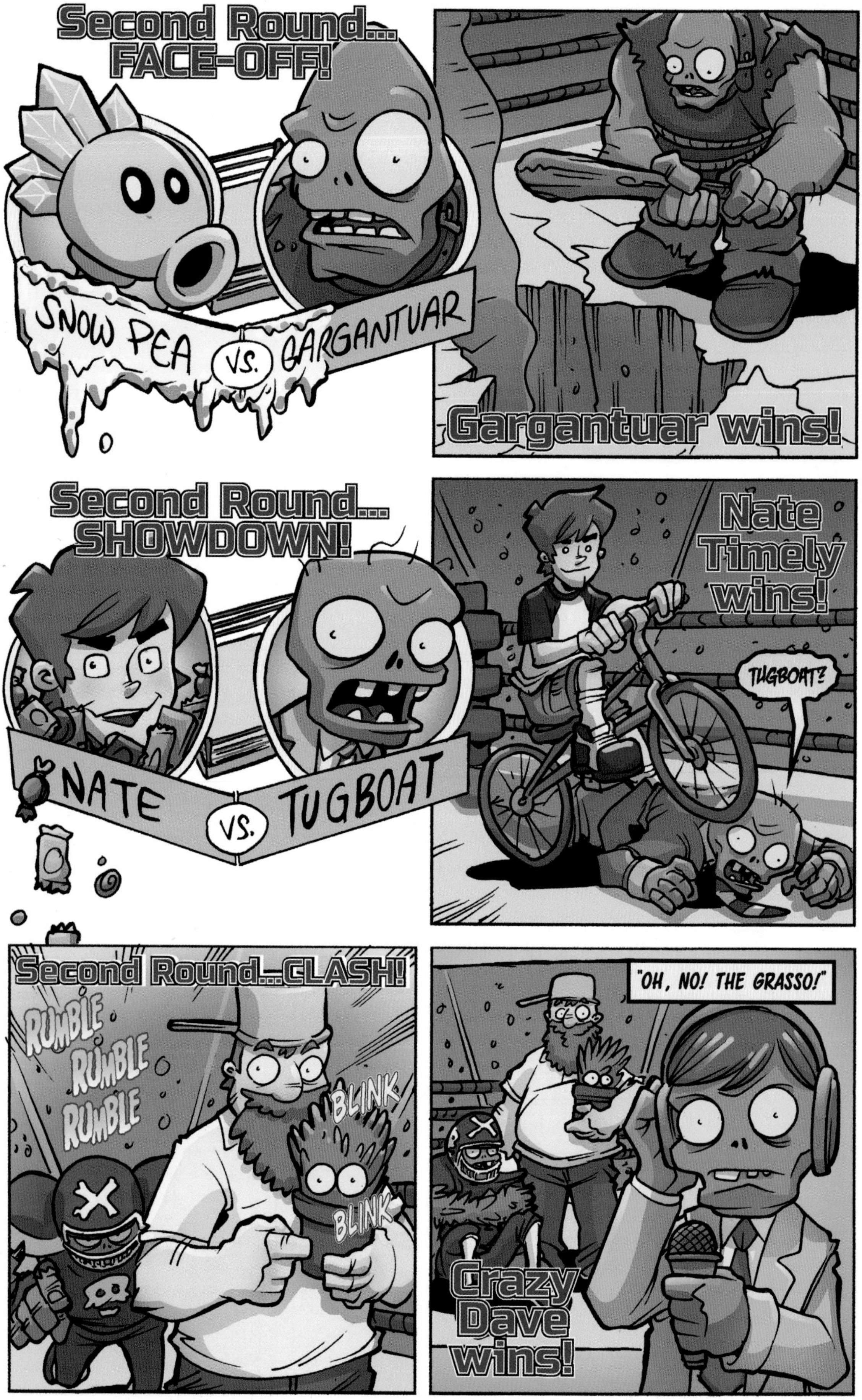
Second Round... FACE-OFF!
SNOW PEA VS. GARGANTUAR
Gargantuar wins!
Second Round... SHOWDOWN!
NATE VS. TUGBOAT
Nate Timely wins!
TUGBOAT?
Second Round...CLASH!
RUMBLE
RUMBLE
RUMBLE
BLINK
BLINK
"OH, NO! THE GRASSO!"
Crazy Dave wins!

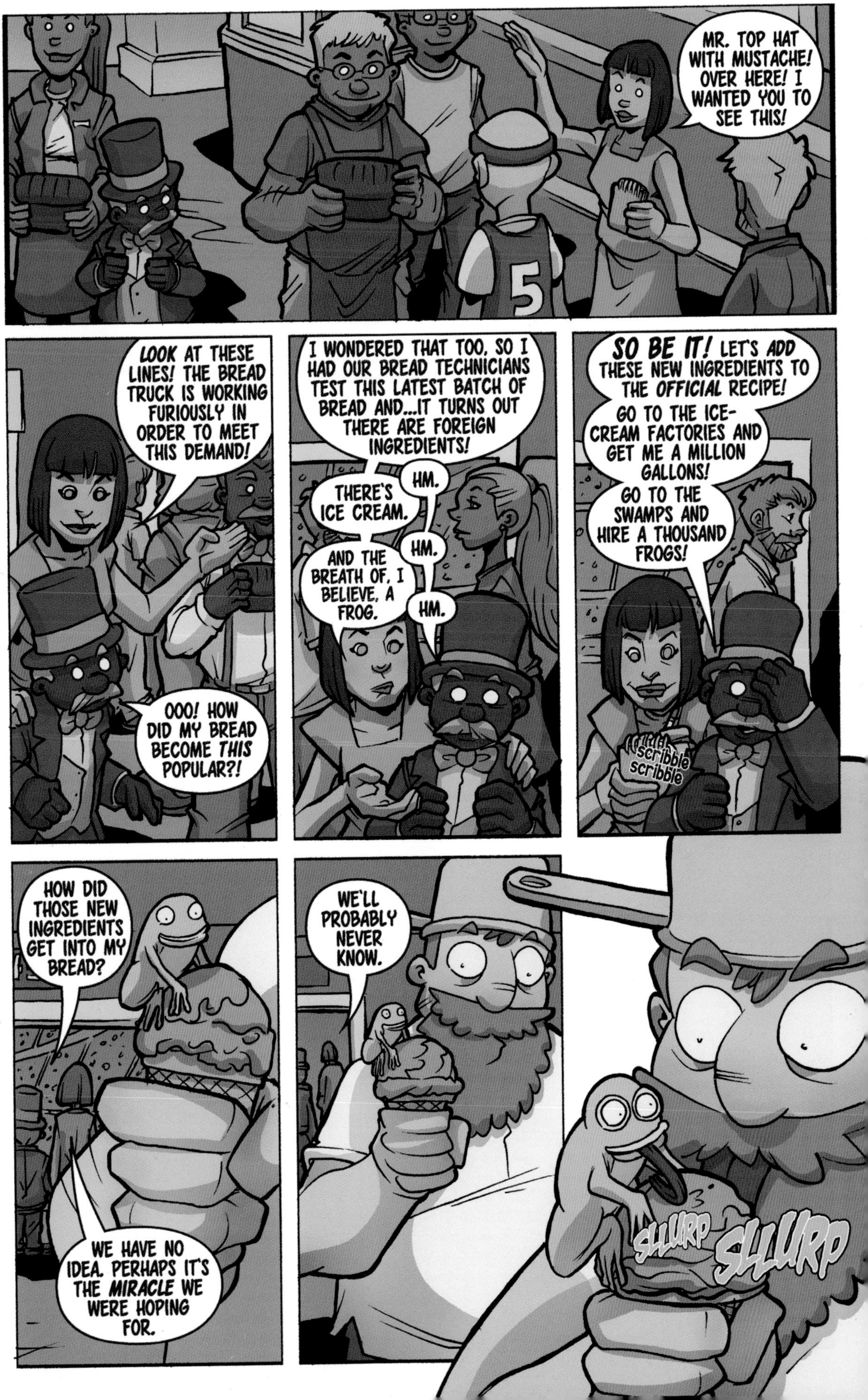
MR. TOP HAT WITH MUSTACHE! OVER HERE! I WANTED YOU TO SEE THIS!
5
LOOK AT THESE LINES! THE BREAD TRUCK IS WORKING FURIOUSLY IN ORDER TO MEET THIS DEMAND!
OOO! HOW DID MY BREAD BECOME THIS POPULAR?!
I WONDERED THAT TOO, SO I HAD OUR BREAD TECHNICIANS TEST THIS LATEST BATCH OF BREAD AND...IT TURNS OUT THERE ARE FOREIGN INGREDIENTS!
THERE'S ICE CREAM.
HM.
AND THE BREATH OF, I BELIEVE, A FROG.
HM.
HM.
SO BE IT! LET'S ADD THESE NEW INGREDIENTS TO THE OFFICIAL RECIPE!
GO TO THE ICE-CREAM FACTORIES AND GET ME A MILLION GALLONS!
GO TO THE SWAMPS AND HIRE A THOUSAND FROGS!
scribble scribble
HOW DID THOSE NEW INGREDIENTS GET INTO MY BREAD?
WE HAVE NO IDEA. PERHAPS IT'S THE MIRACLE WE WERE HOPING FOR.
WE'LL PROBABLY NEVER KNOW.
SLLURP
SLLURP

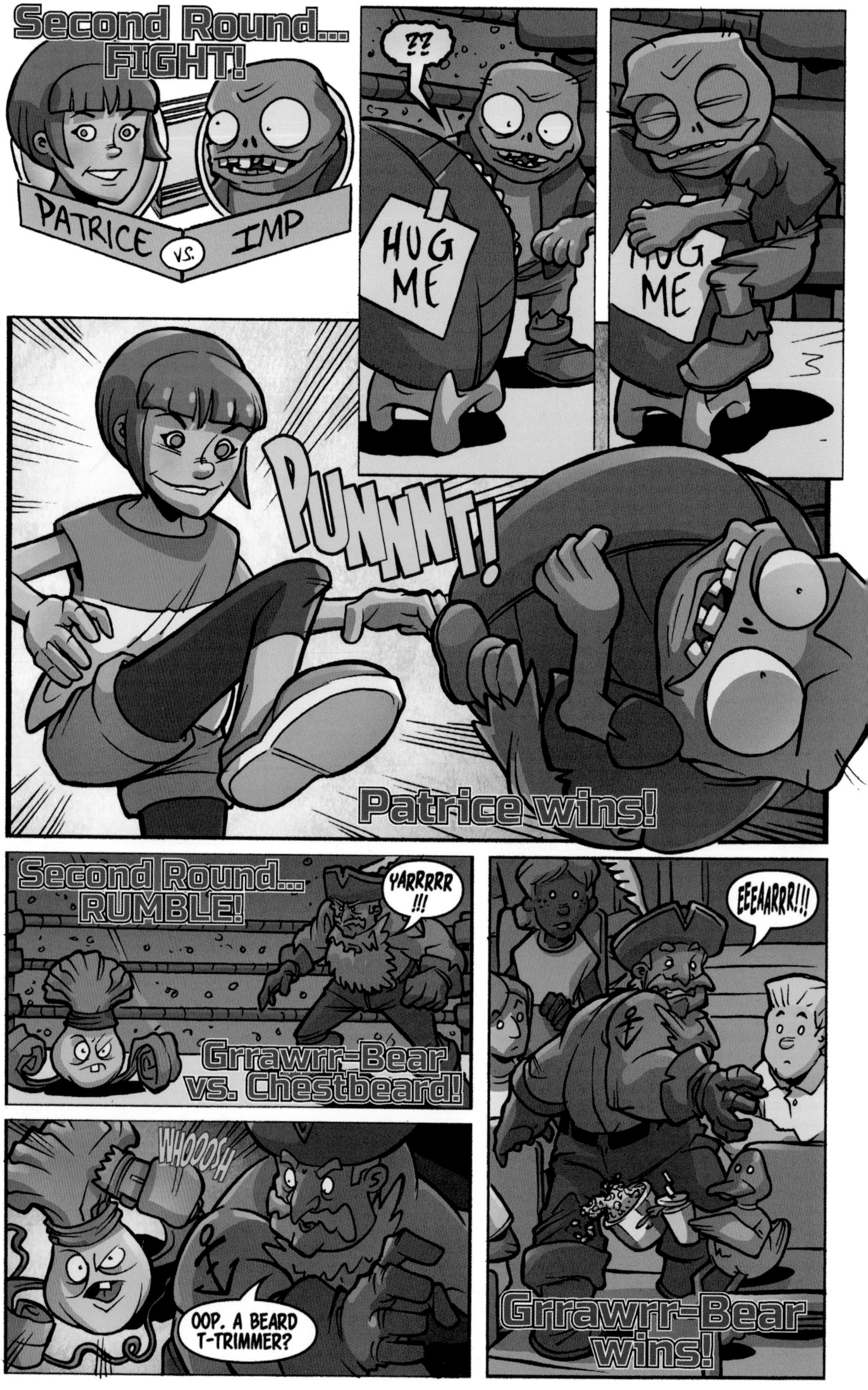
Second Round... FIGHT!
PATRICE
VS.
IMP
??
HUG ME
HUG ME
PUNNNT!
Patrice wins!
Second Round... RUMBLE!
YARRRRR!!!
Grrawrr-Bear vs. Chestbeard!
WHOOOSH
OOP. A BEARD T-TRIMMER?
EEEAARRR!!!
Grrawrr-Bear wins!

AND THEN...

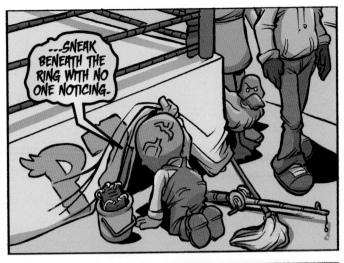

...SNEAK BENEATH THE RING WITH NO ONE NOTICING.

UNSUSPICIOUS CUSTODIAN

THIS TIME, MY PLAN IS FLAWLESS. MY AMAZING CUSTODIAL DISGUISE WILL ALLOW ME TO....

HMM... DARKER IN HERE THAN I THOUGHT IT WOULD BE.

UNSUSPICIOUS CUSTODIAN

CAN'T SEE ANYTHING. NOT SURE WHERE TO PUT THIS BADGUETTE.

LUCKILY, I ALWAYS CARRY MY Z-TECH FLASHLIGHT, SO THAT I CAN CLEARLY SEE....

BLINK BLINK BLINK

...ALL OF THESE EXPLOSIVE MUSHROOMS.

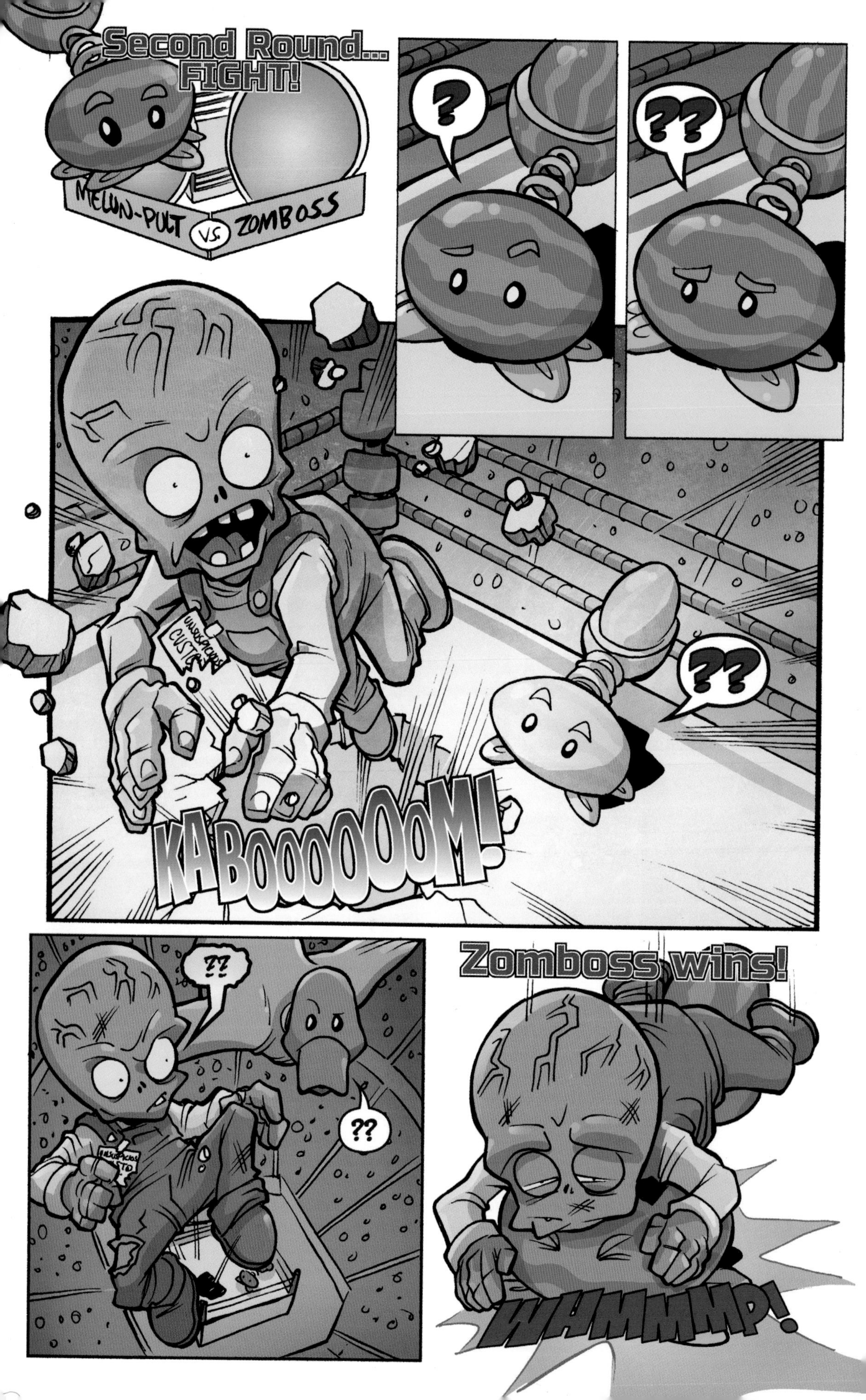
Second Round...
FIGHT!
MELON-PULT
VS.
ZOMBOSS
?
??
KABOOOOOOOM!
??
??
??
Zomboss wins!
WHMMMP!

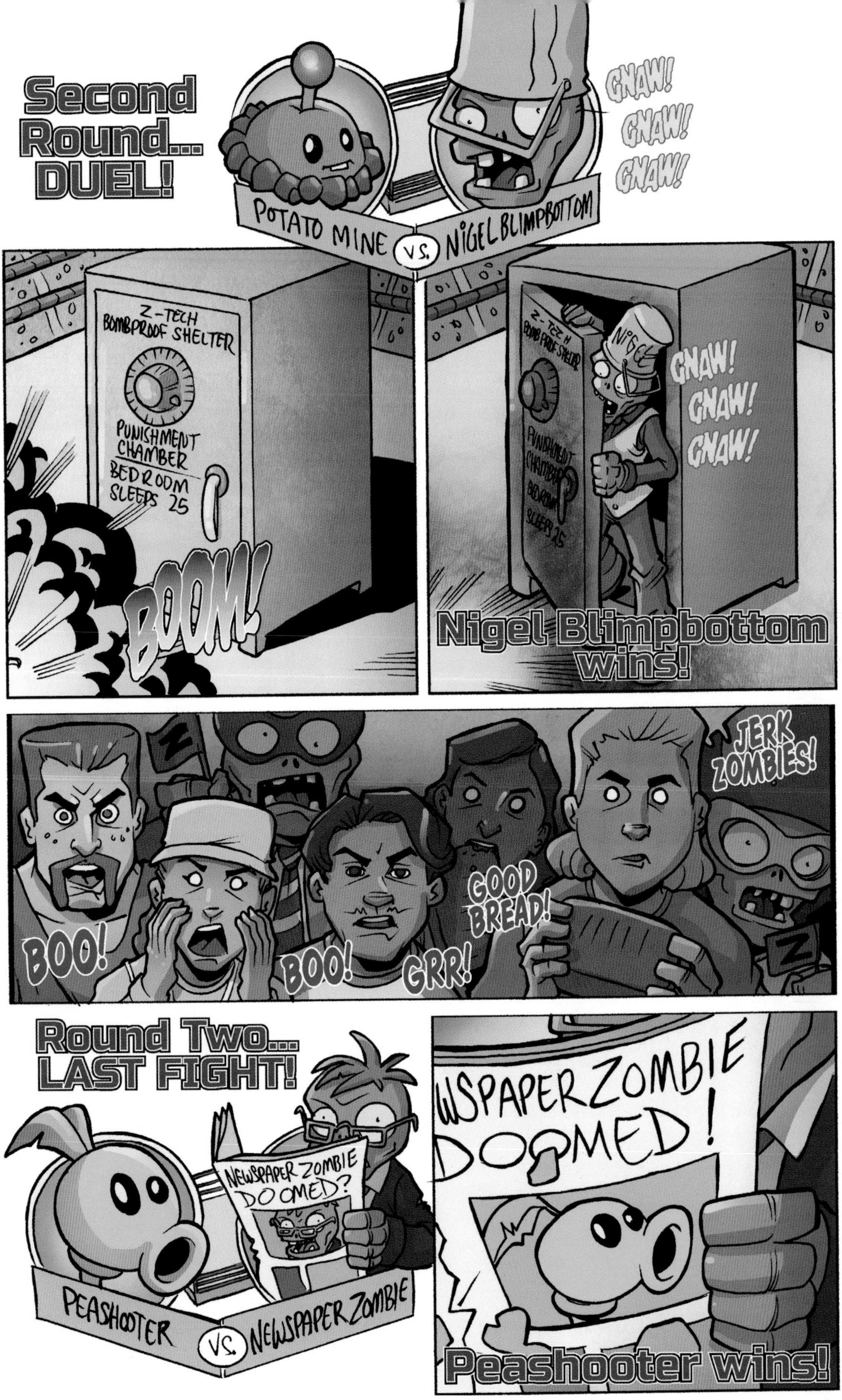
Second Round... DUEL!
GNAW! GNAW! GNAW!
POTATO MINE VS. NIGEL BLIMPBOTTOM
Z-TECH BOMBPROOF SHELTER
PUNISHMENT CHAMBER
BEDROOM SLEEPS 25
BOOM!
NIGEL
GNAW! GNAW! GNAW!
Nigel Blimpbottom wins!
JERK ZOMBIES!
GOOD BREAD!
BOO!
BOO!
GRR!
Round Two... LAST FIGHT!
NEWSPAPER ZOMBIE DOOMED?
PEASHOOTER VS. NEWSPAPER ZOMBIE
WSPAPER ZOMBIE DOOMED!
Peashooter wins!

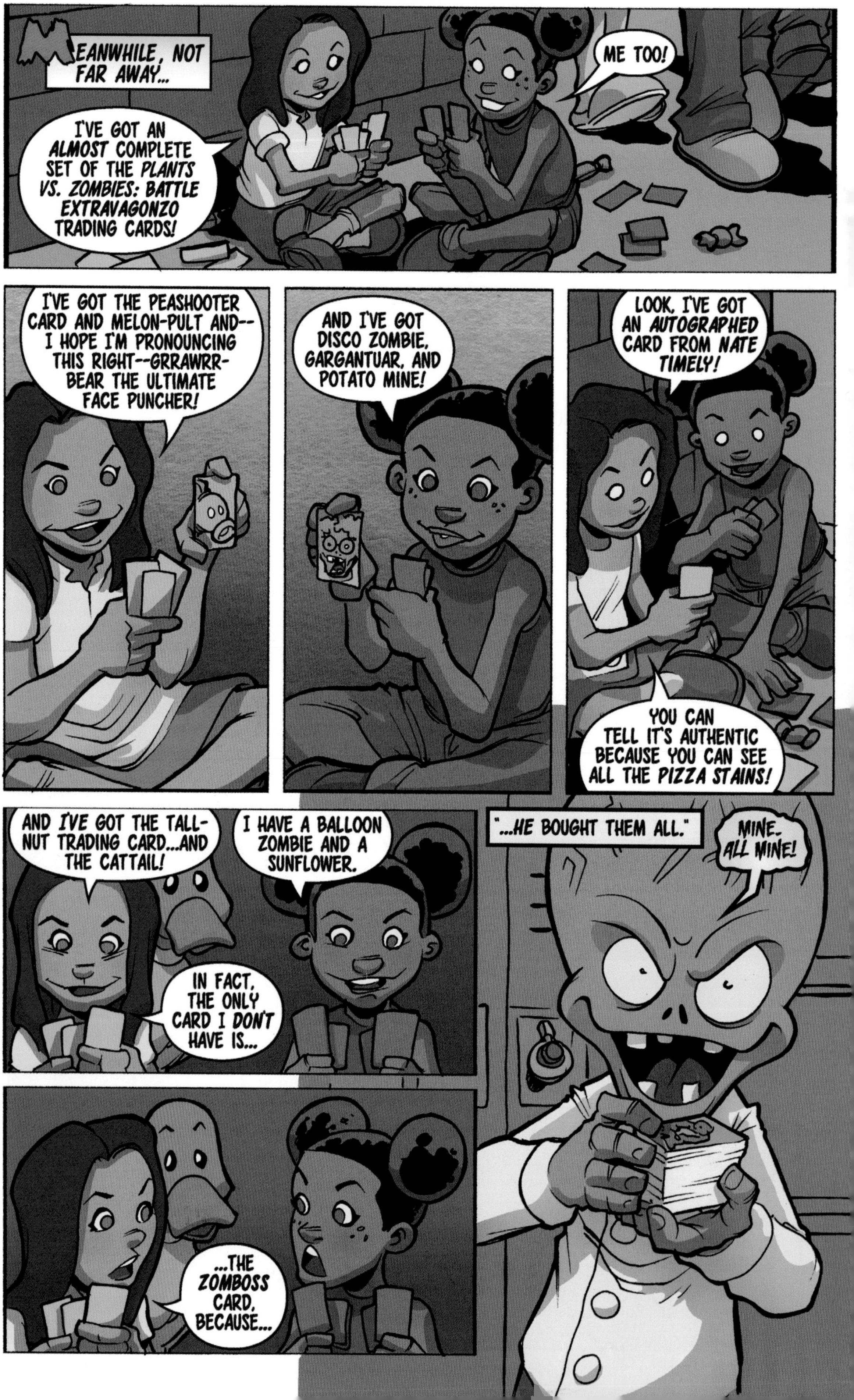
MEANWHILE, NOT FAR AWAY...
I'VE GOT AN ALMOST COMPLETE SET OF THE PLANTS VS. ZOMBIES: BATTLE EXTRAVAGONZO TRADING CARDS!
ME TOO!
I'VE GOT THE PEASHOOTER CARD AND MELON-PULT AND-- I HOPE I'M PRONOUNCING THIS RIGHT--GRRAWRR-BEAR THE ULTIMATE FACE PUNCHER!
AND I'VE GOT DISCO ZOMBIE, GARGANTUAR, AND POTATO MINE!
LOOK, I'VE GOT AN AUTOGRAPHED CARD FROM NATE TIMELY!
YOU CAN TELL IT'S AUTHENTIC BECAUSE YOU CAN SEE ALL THE PIZZA STAINS!
AND I'VE GOT THE TALL-NUT TRADING CARD...AND THE CATTAIL!
I HAVE A BALLOON ZOMBIE AND A SUNFLOWER.
IN FACT, THE ONLY CARD I DON'T HAVE IS...
...THE ZOMBOSS CARD, BECAUSE...
"...HE BOUGHT THEM ALL."
MINE. ALL MINE!

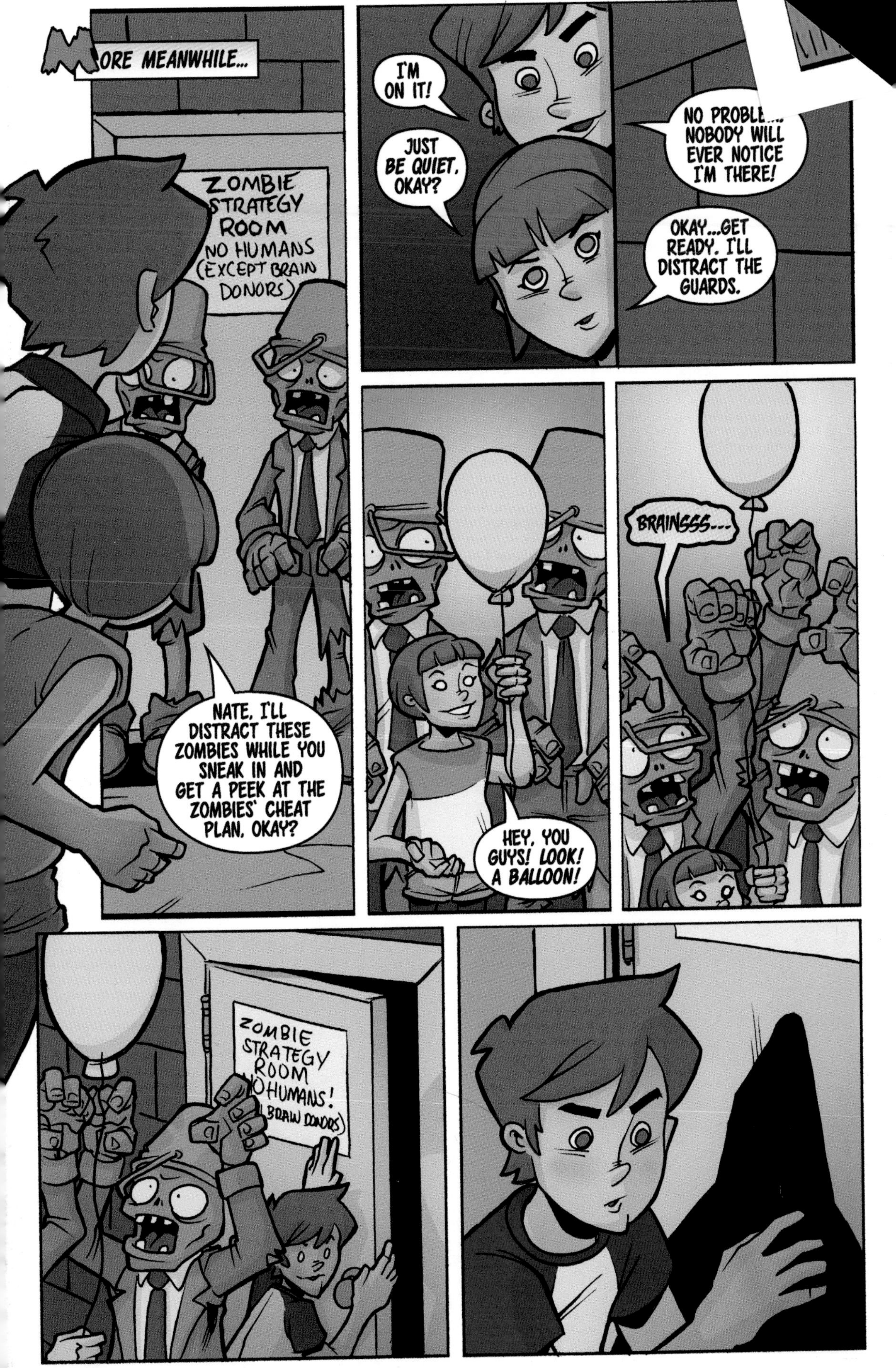
MORE MEANWHILE...
ZOMBIE STRATEGY ROOM NO HUMANS (EXCEPT BRAIN DONORS)
NATE, I'LL DISTRACT THESE ZOMBIES WHILE YOU SNEAK IN AND GET A PEEK AT THE ZOMBIES' CHEAT PLAN, OKAY?
I'M ON IT!
JUST BE QUIET, OKAY?
NO PROBLE... NOBODY WILL EVER NOTICE I'M THERE!
OKAY...GET READY. I'LL DISTRACT THE GUARDS.
HEY, YOU GUYS! LOOK! A BALLOON!
BRAINSSS...
ZOMBIE STRATEGY ROOM
HUMANS!

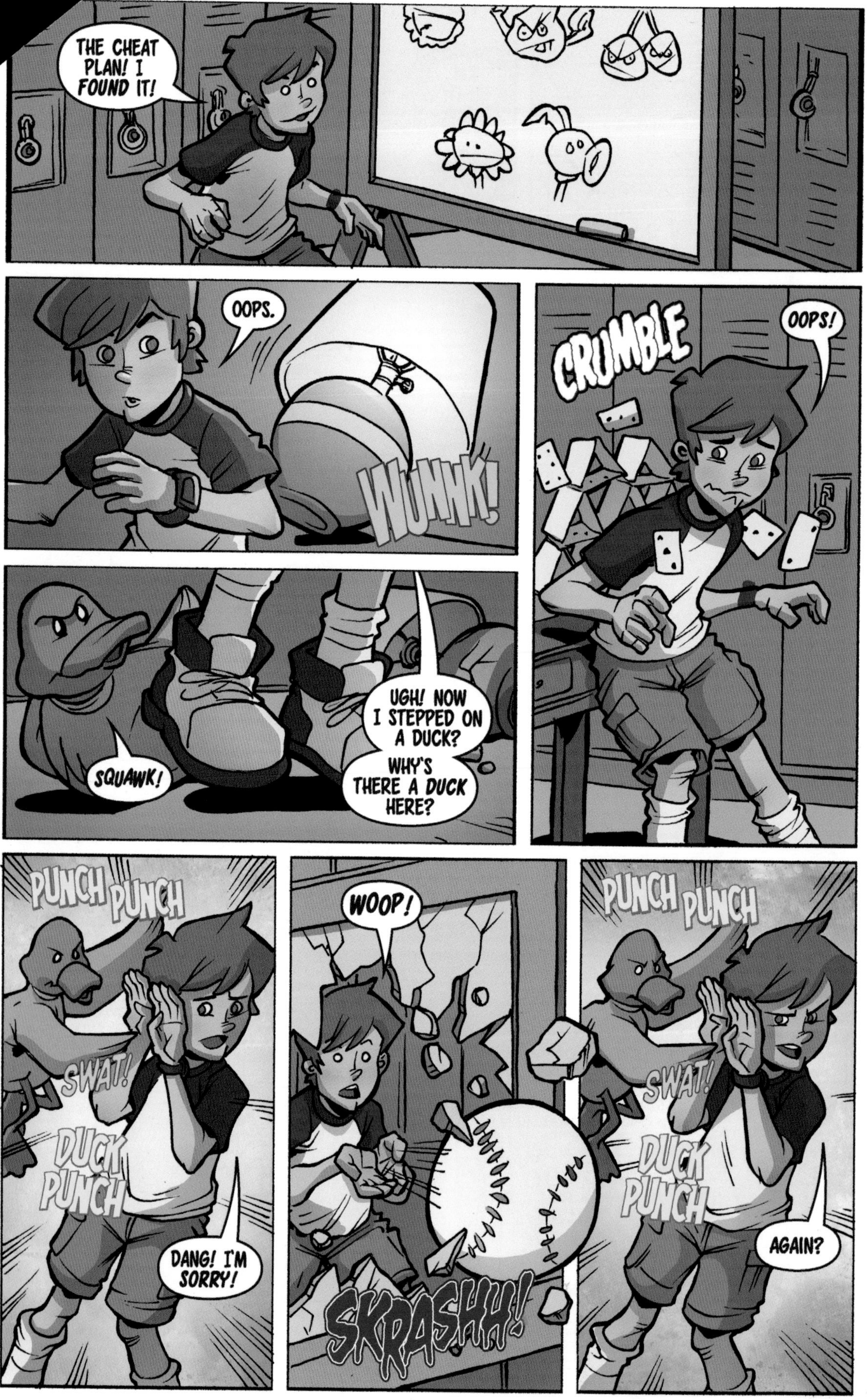

THE CHEAT PLAN! I FOUND IT!
OOPS.
WUNNK!
CRUMBLE
OOPS!
SQUAWK!
UGH! NOW I STEPPED ON A DUCK?
WHY'S THERE A DUCK HERE?
PUNCH PUNCH
SWAT!
DUCK PUNCH
DANG! I'M SORRY!
WOOP!
SKRASHH!
PUNCH PUNCH
SWAT!
DUCK PUNCH
AGAIN?

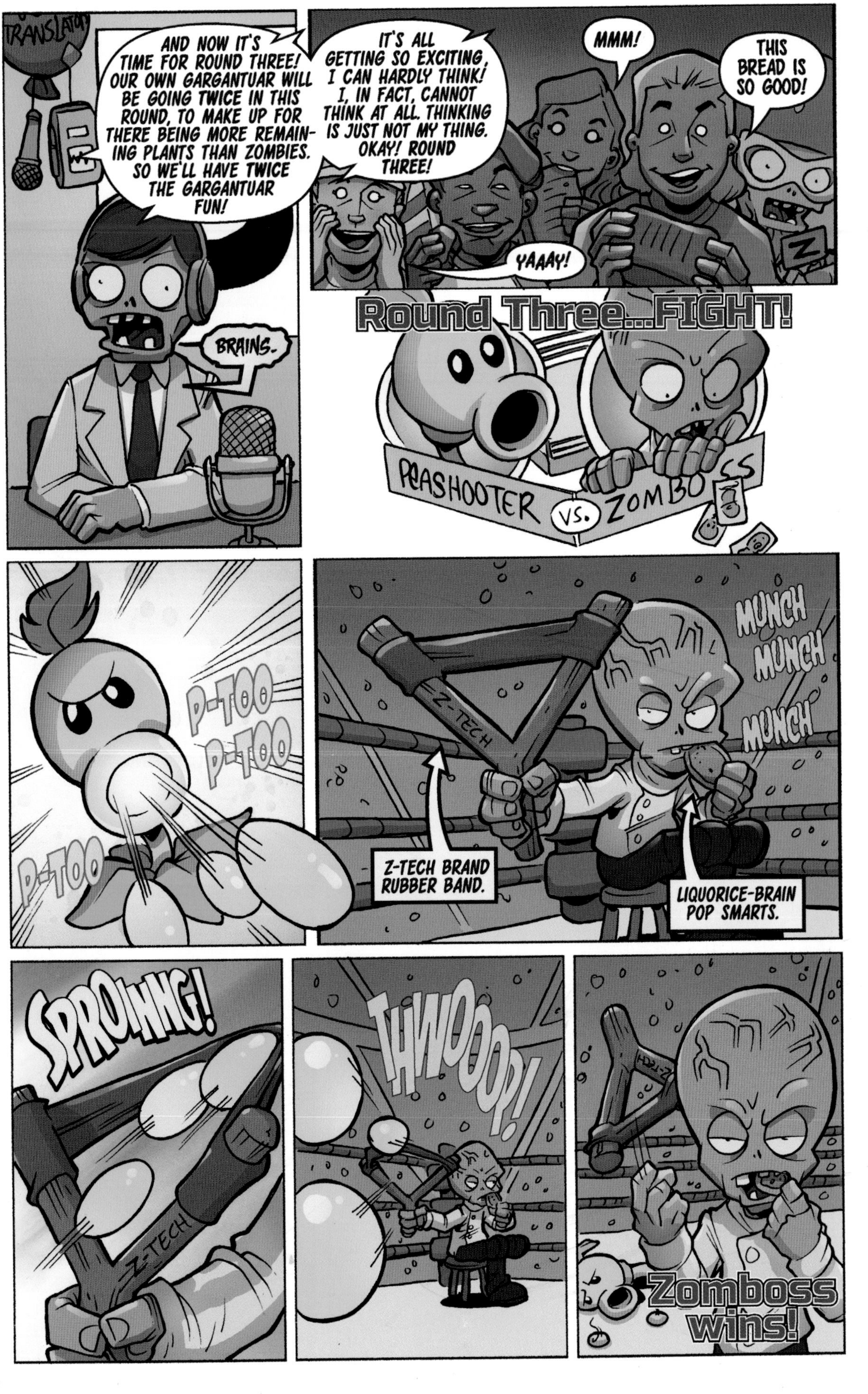
TRANSLATION
AND NOW IT'S TIME FOR ROUND THREE! OUR OWN GARGANTUAR WILL BE GOING TWICE IN THIS ROUND, TO MAKE UP FOR THERE BEING MORE REMAIN-ING PLANTS THAN ZOMBIES. SO WE'LL HAVE TWICE THE GARGANTUAR FUN!
BRAINS.
IT'S ALL GETTING SO EXCITING, I CAN HARDLY THINK! I, IN FACT, CANNOT THINK AT ALL. THINKING IS JUST NOT MY THING. OKAY! ROUND THREE!
MMM!
THIS BREAD IS SO GOOD!
YAAAY!
Round Three...FIGHT!
PEASHOOTER VS. ZOMBOSS
P-TOO
P-TOO
P-TOO
Z-TECH
MUNCH
MUNCH
MUNCH
Z-TECH BRAND RUBBER BAND.
LIQUORICE-BRAIN POP SMARTS.
SPROINNG!
Z-TECH
THWOOOP!
Zomboss wins!

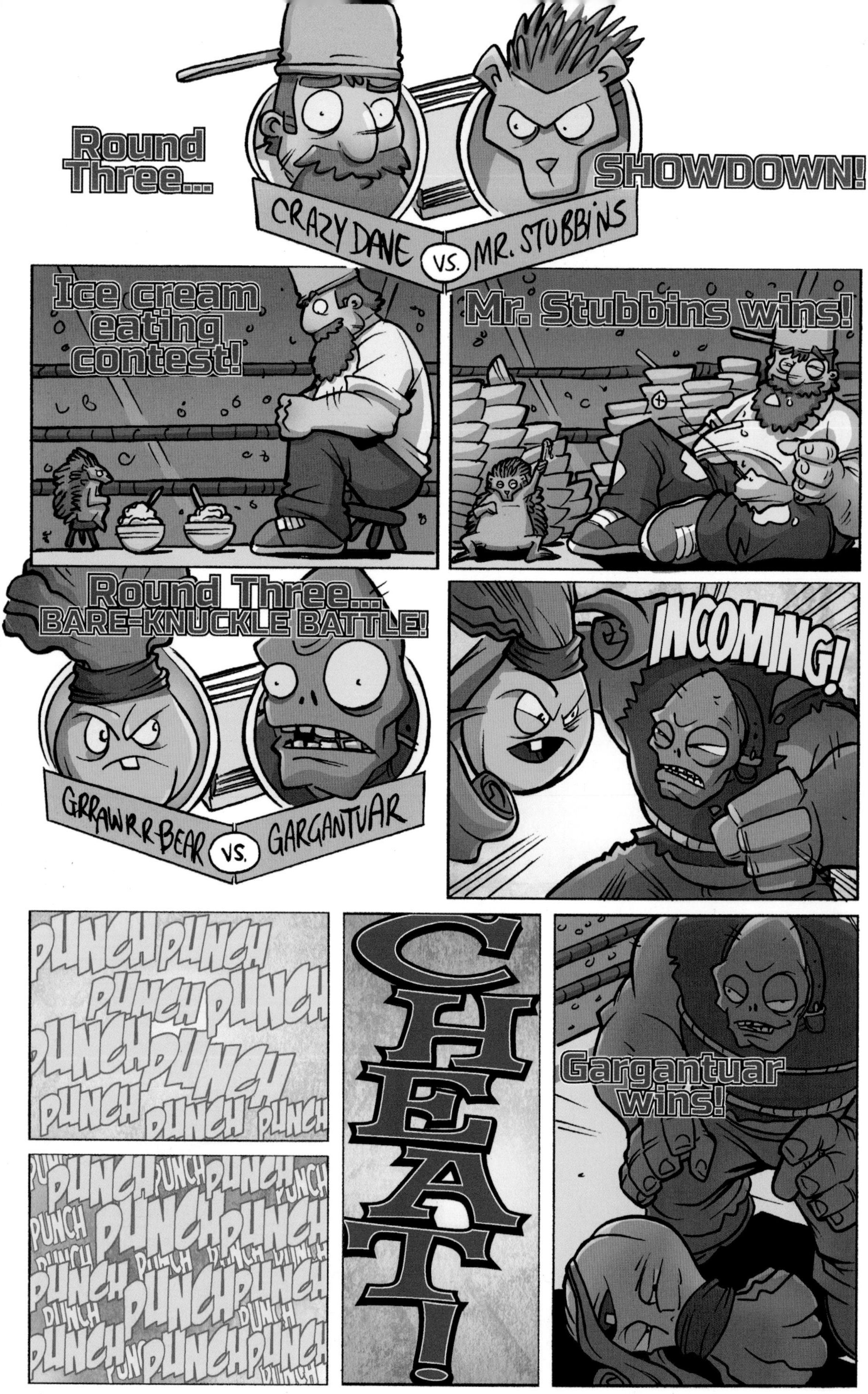
Round Three...
CRAZY DAVE
VS.
MR. STUBBINS
SHOWDOWN!
Ice cream eating contest!
Mr. Stubbins wins!
Round Three...
BARE-KNUCKLE BATTLE!
GRRAWRR-BEAR
VS.
GARGANTUAR
INCOMING!
PUNCH PUNCH PUNCH PUNCH PUNCH PUNCH PUNCH PUNCH PUNCH
PUNCH PUNCH PUNCH PUNCH PUNCH PUNCH PUNCH PUNCH PUNCH PUNCH PUNCH PUNCH PUNCH PUNCH
CHEAT!
Gargantuar wins!

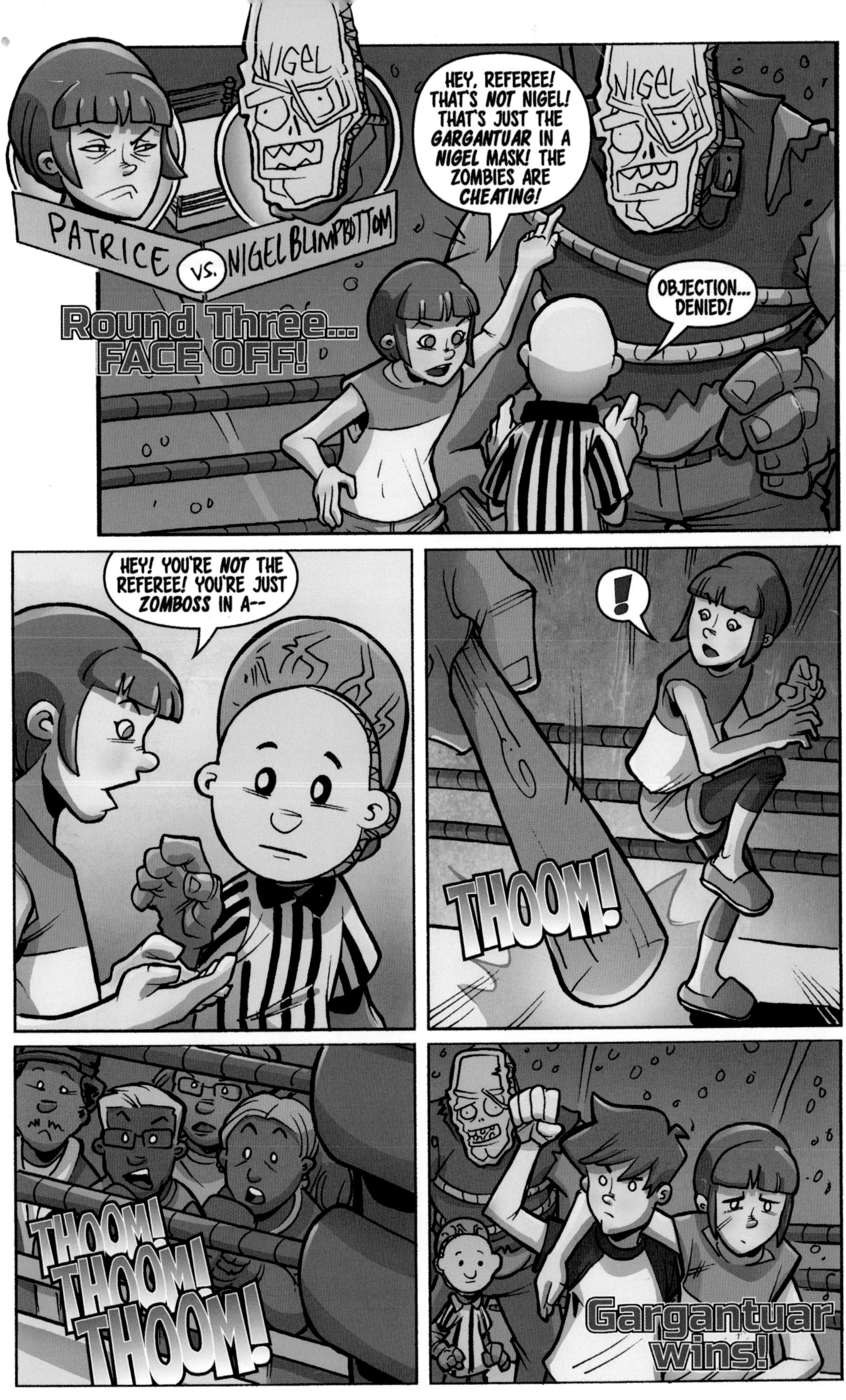
PATRICE
VS.
NIGEL BLIMPBOTTOM
Round Three... FACE OFF!
HEY, REFEREE! THAT'S NOT NIGEL! THAT'S JUST THE GARGANTUAR IN A NIGEL MASK! THE ZOMBIES ARE CHEATING!
OBJECTION... DENIED!
HEY! YOU'RE NOT THE REFEREE! YOU'RE JUST ZOMBOSS IN A--
!
THOOM!
THOOM! THOOM! THOOM!
Gargantuar wins!

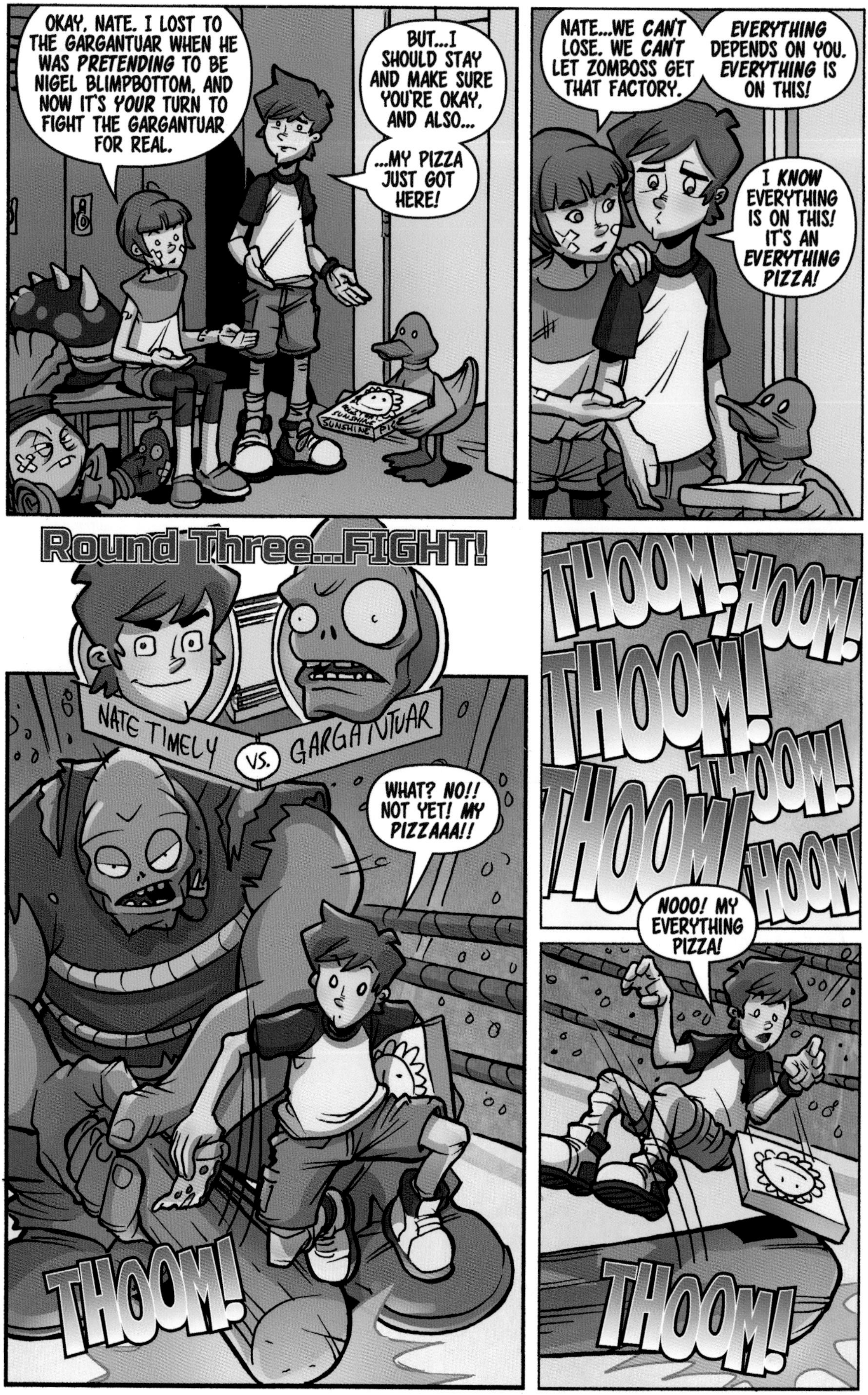

OKAY, NATE. I LOST TO THE GARGANTUAR WHEN HE WAS *PRETENDING* TO BE NIGEL BLIMPBOTTOM, AND NOW IT'S *YOUR* TURN TO FIGHT THE GARGANTUAR FOR REAL.
BUT...I SHOULD STAY AND MAKE SURE YOU'RE OKAY, AND ALSO...
...MY PIZZA JUST GOT HERE!
NATE...WE *CAN'T* LOSE. WE *CAN'T* LET ZOMBOSS GET THAT FACTORY.
EVERYTHING DEPENDS ON YOU. *EVERYTHING* IS ON THIS!
I *KNOW* EVERYTHING IS ON THIS! IT'S AN *EVERYTHING* PIZZA!
Round Three...FIGHT!
NATE TIMELY
VS.
GARGANTUAR
WHAT? *NO!!* NOT YET! *MY PIZZAAA!!*
THOOM!
THOOM! THOOM! THOOM! THOOM! THOOM! THOOM!
NOOO! MY EVERYTHING PIZZA!
THOOM!

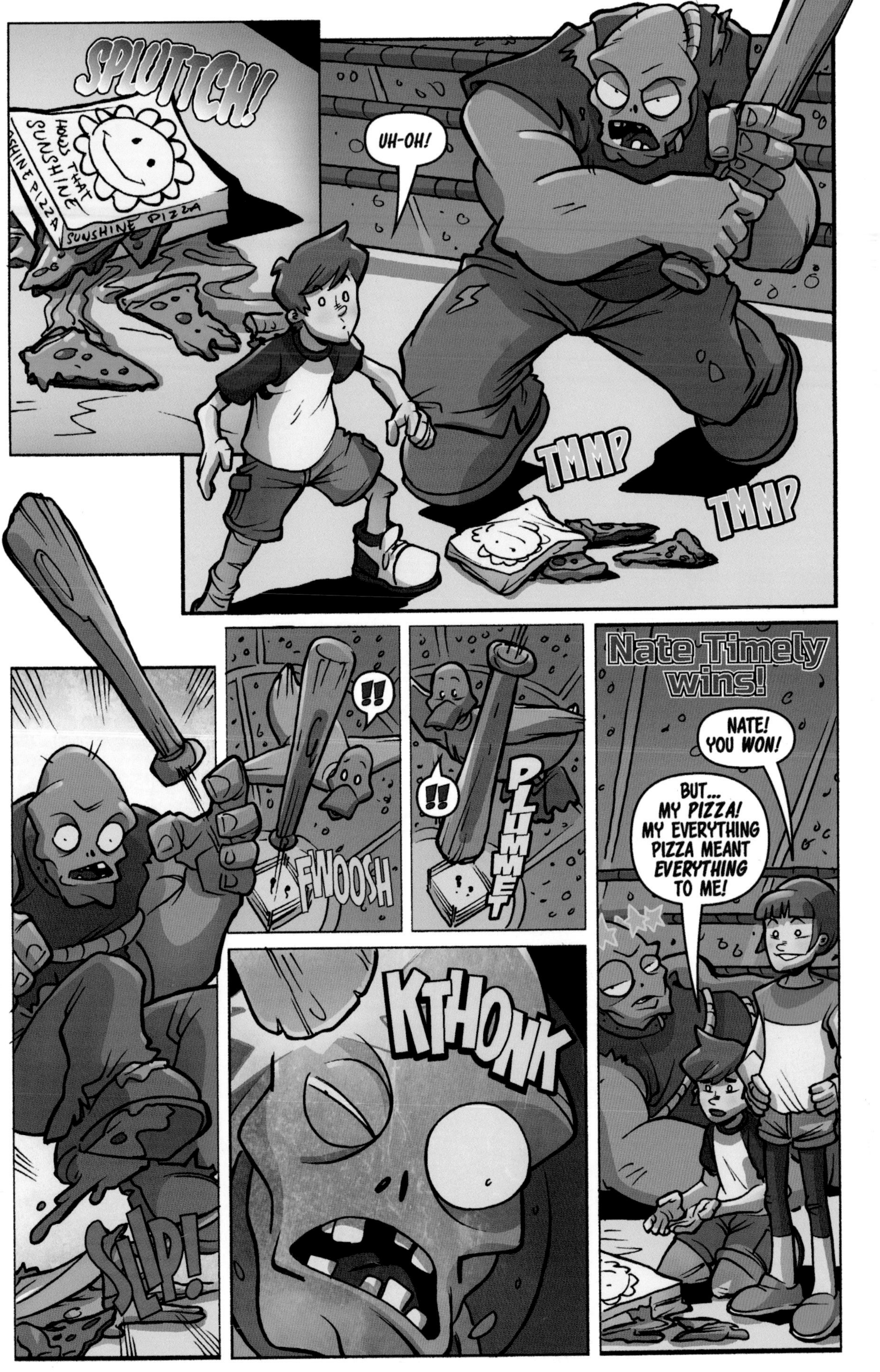
SPLUTTCH!
HOWS THAT SUNSHINE
SUNSHINE PIZZA
UH-OH!
TMMP
TMMP
!!
FWOOSH
!!
PLUMMET
SLIP!
KTHONK
Nate Timely wins!
NATE! YOU WON!
BUT... MY PIZZA! MY EVERYTHING PIZZA MEANT EVERYTHING TO ME!

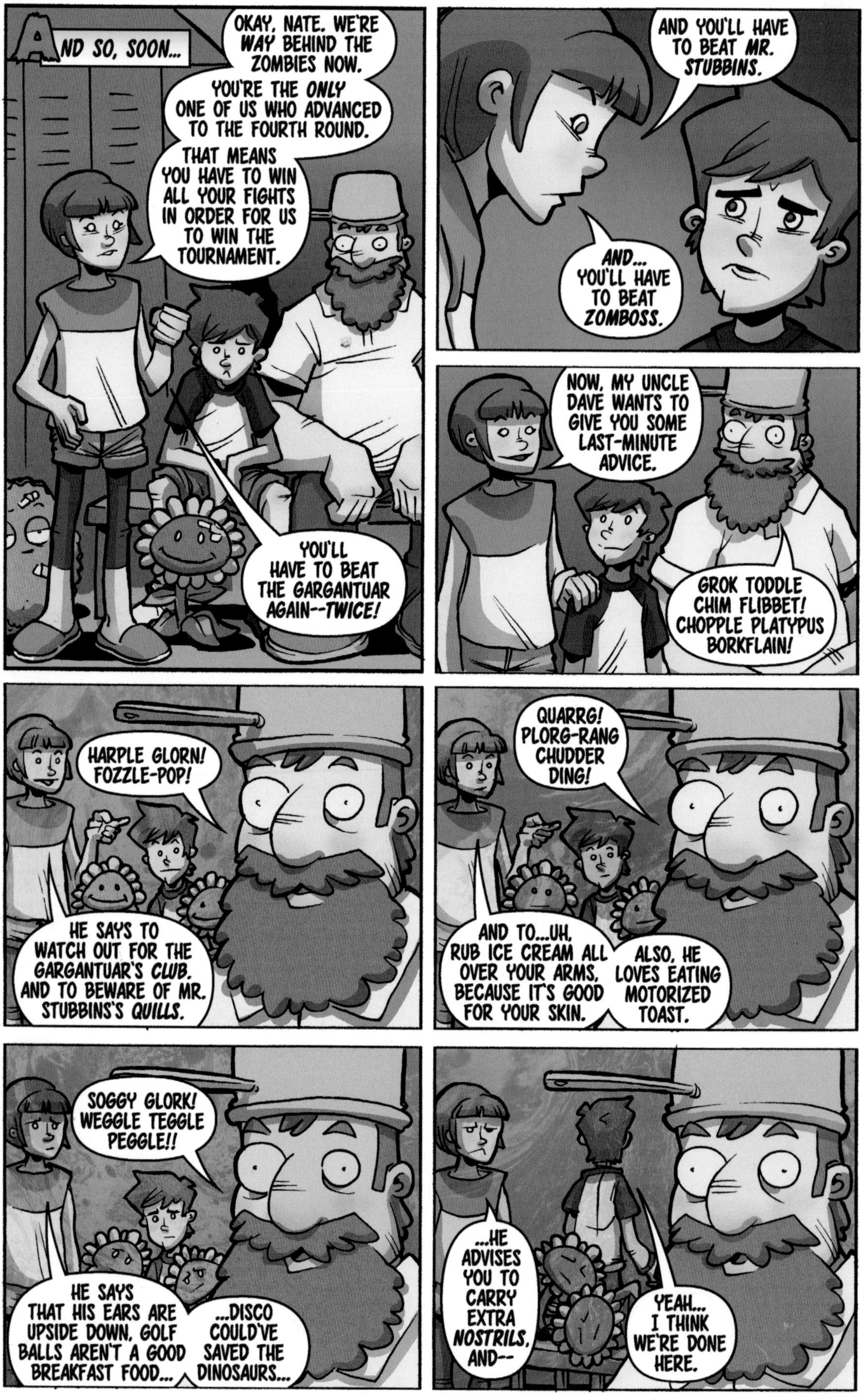
AND SO, SOON...
OKAY, NATE. WE'RE WAY BEHIND THE ZOMBIES NOW.
YOU'RE THE ONLY ONE OF US WHO ADVANCED TO THE FOURTH ROUND.
THAT MEANS YOU HAVE TO WIN ALL YOUR FIGHTS IN ORDER FOR US TO WIN THE TOURNAMENT.
YOU'LL HAVE TO BEAT THE GARGANTUAR AGAIN--TWICE!
AND YOU'LL HAVE TO BEAT MR. STUBBINS.
AND... YOU'LL HAVE TO BEAT ZOMBOSS.
NOW, MY UNCLE DAVE WANTS TO GIVE YOU SOME LAST-MINUTE ADVICE.
GROK TODDLE CHIM FLIBBET! CHOPPLE PLATYPUS BORKFLAIN!
HARPLE GLORN! FOZZLE-POP!
HE SAYS TO WATCH OUT FOR THE GARGANTUAR'S CLUB. AND TO BEWARE OF MR. STUBBINS'S QUILLS.
QUARRG! PLORG-RANG CHUDDER DING!
AND TO...UH, RUB ICE CREAM ALL OVER YOUR ARMS, BECAUSE IT'S GOOD FOR YOUR SKIN.
ALSO, HE LOVES EATING MOTORIZED TOAST.
SOGGY GLORK! WEGGLE TEGGLE PEGGLE!!
HE SAYS THAT HIS EARS ARE UPSIDE DOWN, GOLF BALLS AREN'T A GOOD BREAKFAST FOOD...
...DISCO COULD'VE SAVED THE DINOSAURS...
...HE ADVISES YOU TO CARRY EXTRA NOSTRILS, AND--
YEAH... I THINK WE'RE DONE HERE.

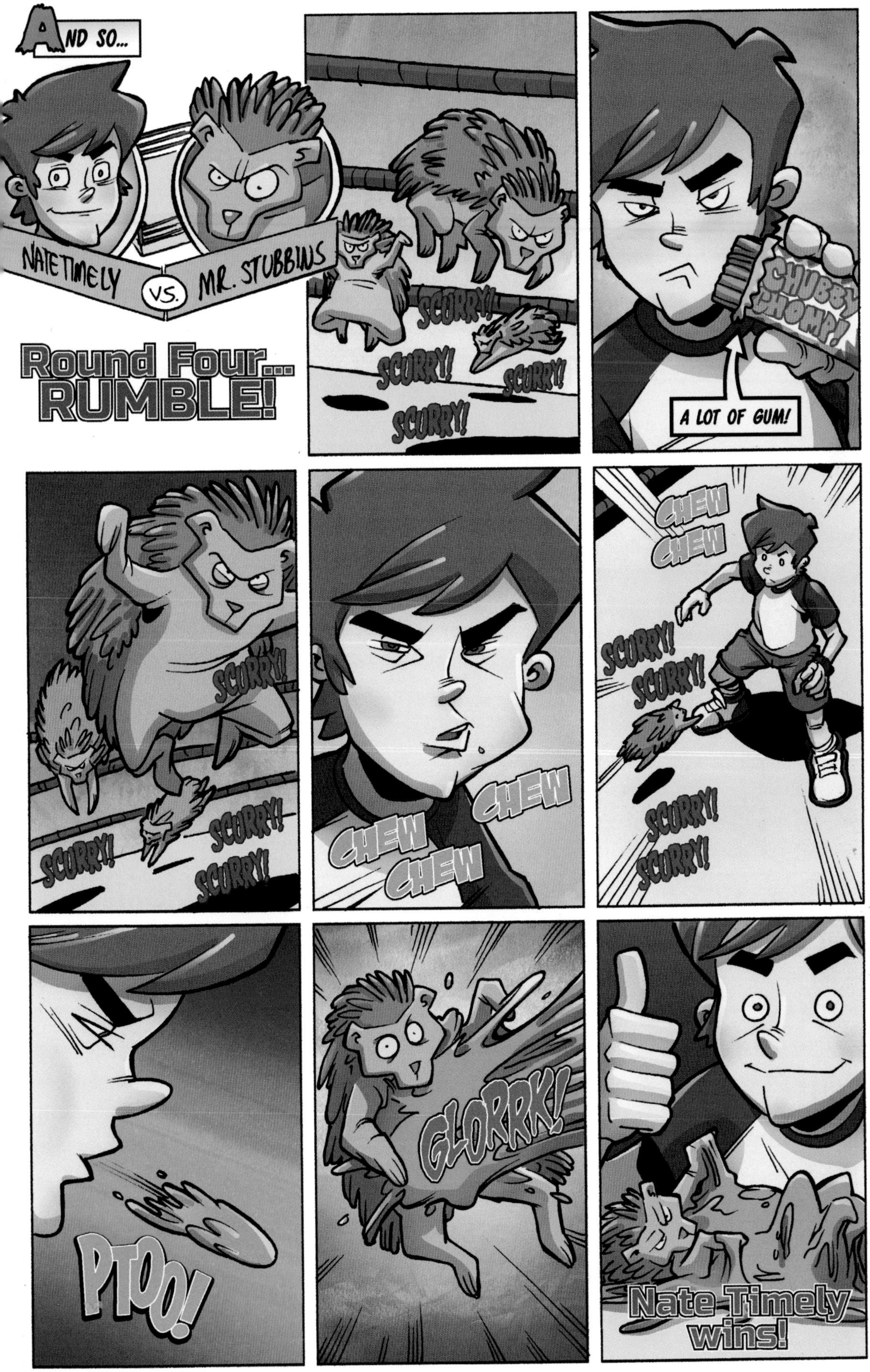
AND SO...
NATE TIMELY
VS.
MR. STUBBINS
Round Four... RUMBLE!
SCURRY!
SCURRY!
SCURRY!
SCURRY!
CHUBBY CHOMP!
A LOT OF GUM!
SCURRY!
SCURRY!
SCURRY!
SCURRY!
CHEW
CHEW
CHEW
CHEW
CHEW
SCURRY!
SCURRY!
SCURRY!
SCURRY!
PTOO!
GLORRK!
Nate Timely wins!

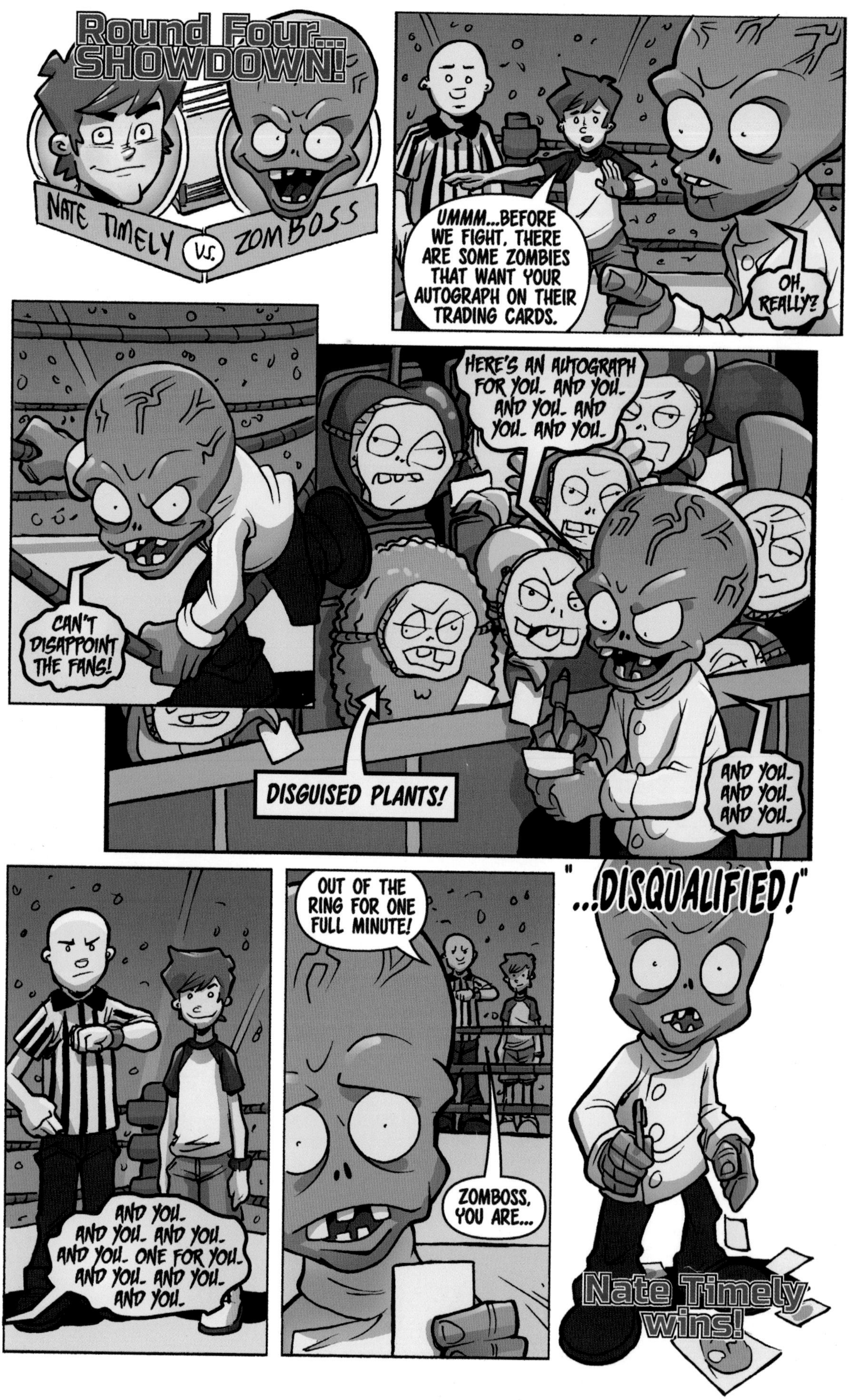
Round Four... SHOWDOWN!
NATE TIMELY
VS.
ZOMBOSS
UMMM...BEFORE WE FIGHT, THERE ARE SOME ZOMBIES THAT WANT YOUR AUTOGRAPH ON THEIR TRADING CARDS.
OH, REALLY?
CAN'T DISAPPOINT THE FANS!
HERE'S AN AUTOGRAPH FOR YOU. AND YOU. AND YOU. AND YOU. AND YOU.
AND YOU. AND YOU. AND YOU.
DISGUISED PLANTS!
AND YOU. AND YOU. AND YOU. AND YOU. ONE FOR YOU. AND YOU. AND YOU. AND YOU.
OUT OF THE RING FOR ONE FULL MINUTE!
ZOMBOSS, YOU ARE...
"...DISQUALIFIED!"
Nate Timely wins!

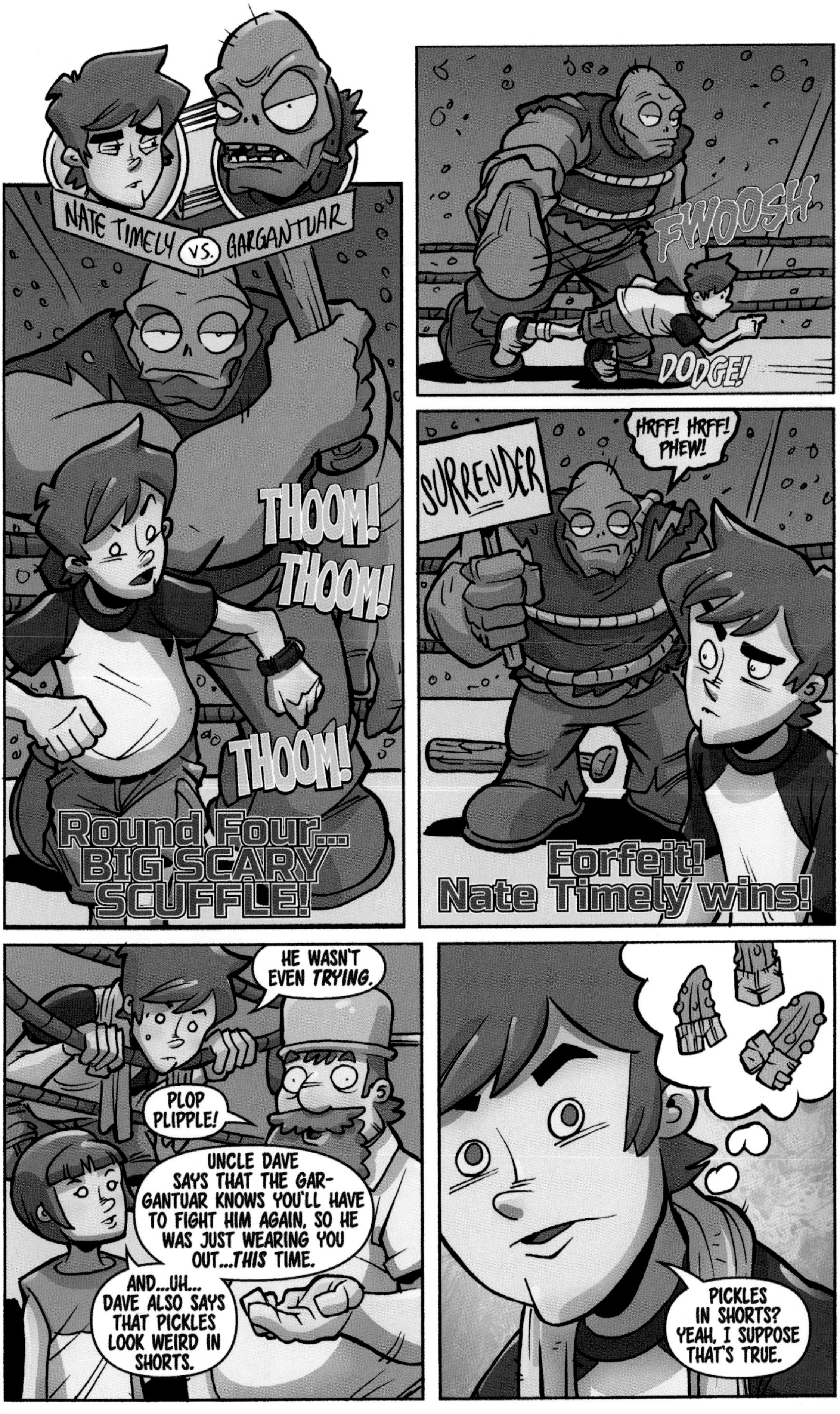

NATE TIMELY VS. GARGANTUAR
THOOM!
THOOM!
THOOM!
Round Four... BIG SCARY SCUFFLE!
FWOOSH
DODGE!
SURRENDER
HRFF! HRFF! PHEW!
Forfeit! Nate Timely wins!
HE WASN'T EVEN TRYING.
PLOP PLIPPLE!
UNCLE DAVE SAYS THAT THE GAR-GANTUAR KNOWS YOU'LL HAVE TO FIGHT HIM AGAIN, SO HE WAS JUST WEARING YOU OUT...THIS TIME.
AND...UH... DAVE ALSO SAYS THAT PICKLES LOOK WEIRD IN SHORTS.
PICKLES IN SHORTS? YEAH, I SUPPOSE THAT'S TRUE.

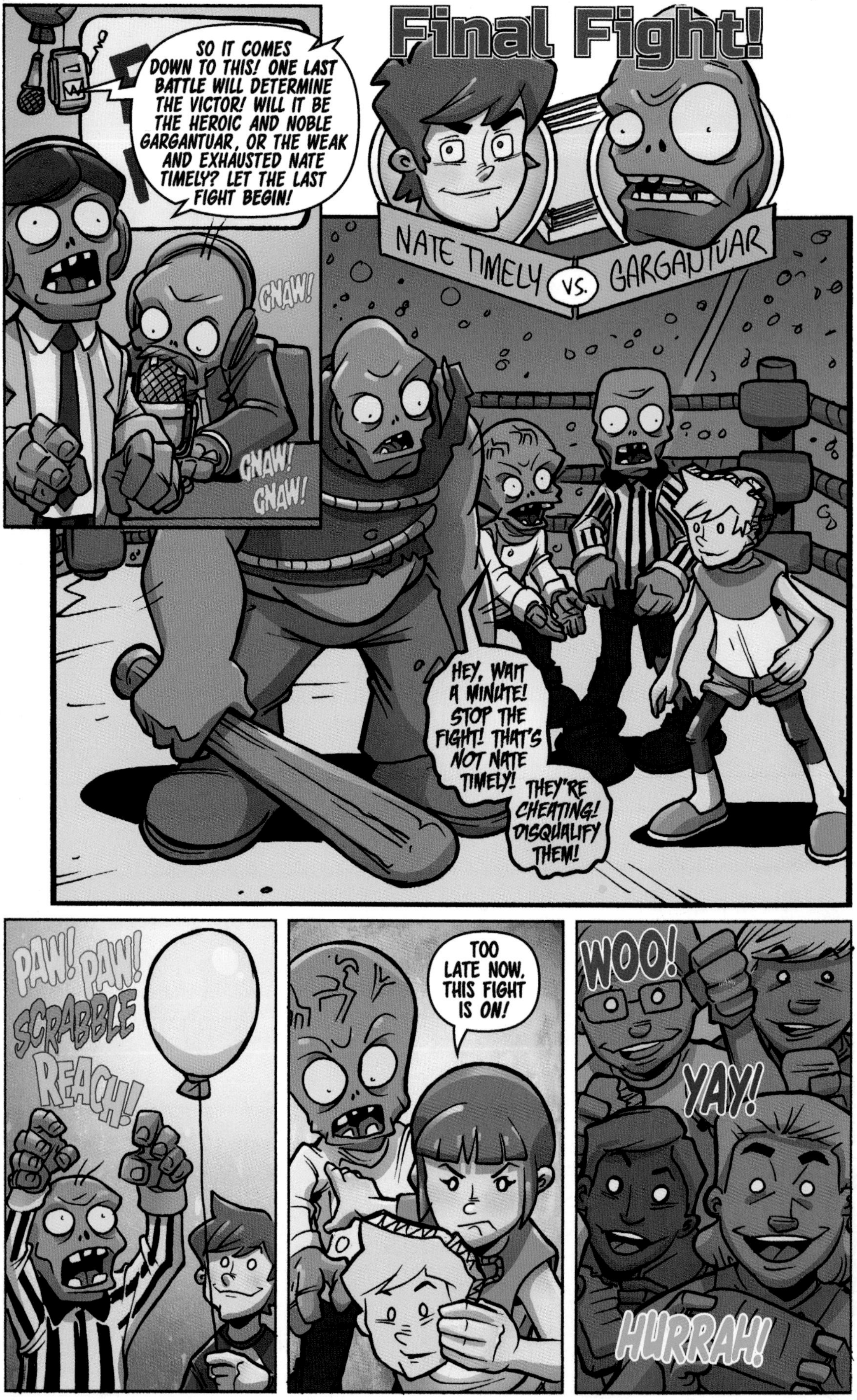
Final Fight!
SO IT COMES DOWN TO THIS! ONE LAST BATTLE WILL DETERMINE THE VICTOR! WILL IT BE THE HEROIC AND NOBLE GARGANTUAR, OR THE WEAK AND EXHAUSTED NATE TIMELY? LET THE LAST FIGHT BEGIN!
GNAW!
GNAW! GNAW!
NATE TIMELY VS. GARGANTUAR
HEY, WAIT A MINUTE! STOP THE FIGHT! THAT'S NOT NATE TIMELY!
THEY'RE CHEATING! DISQUALIFY THEM!
PAW! PAW! SCRABBLE REACH!
TOO LATE NOW, THIS FIGHT IS ON!
WOO!
YAY!
HURRAH!

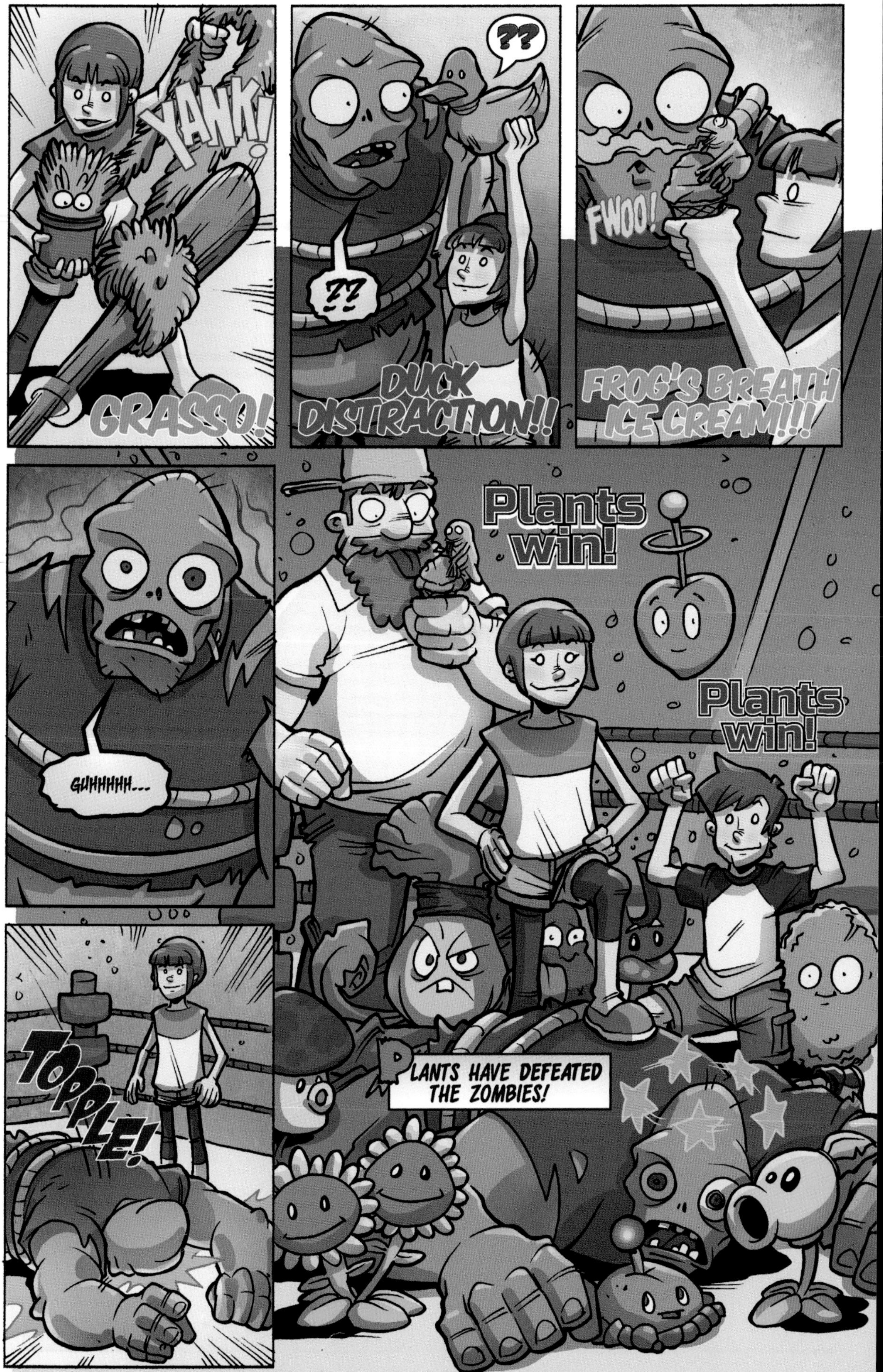
YANK!
GRASSO!
??
??
DUCK DISTRACTION!!
FWOO!
FROG'S BREATH ICE CREAM!!!
GUHHHHH...
Plants win!
Plants win!
TOPPLE!
PLANTS HAVE DEFEATED THE ZOMBIES!

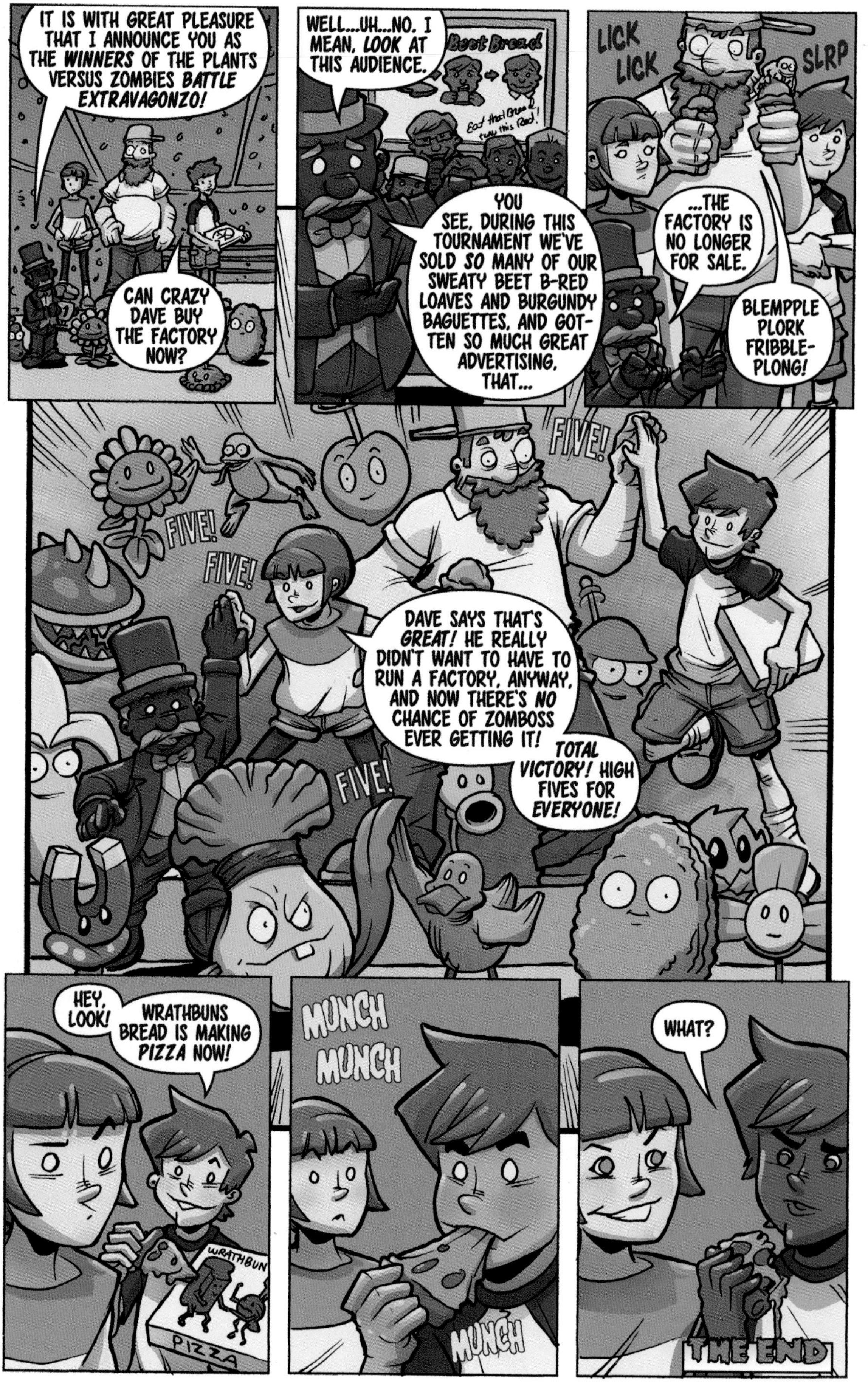

IT IS WITH GREAT PLEASURE THAT I ANNOUNCE YOU AS THE WINNERS OF THE PLANTS VERSUS ZOMBIES BATTLE EXTRAVAGONZO!
CAN CRAZY DAVE BUY THE FACTORY NOW?
WELL...UH...NO. I MEAN, LOOK AT THIS AUDIENCE.
Beet Bread
YOU SEE, DURING THIS TOURNAMENT WE'VE SOLD SO MANY OF OUR SWEATY BEET B-RED LOAVES AND BURGUNDY BAGUETTES, AND GOTTEN SO MUCH GREAT ADVERTISING, THAT...
LICK LICK
SLRP
...THE FACTORY IS NO LONGER FOR SALE.
BLEMPPLE PLORK FRIBBLE-PLONG!
FIVE!
FIVE!
FIVE!
DAVE SAYS THAT'S GREAT! HE REALLY DIDN'T WANT TO HAVE TO RUN A FACTORY, ANYWAY, AND NOW THERE'S NO CHANCE OF ZOMBOSS EVER GETTING IT!
FIVE!
TOTAL VICTORY! HIGH FIVES FOR EVERYONE!
HEY, LOOK!
WRATHBUNS BREAD IS MAKING PIZZA NOW!
WRATHBUN
PIZZA
MUNCH
MUNCH
MUNCH
WHAT?
THE END